THE ADVENTURE OF THE INJURED CABMAN

AND A SHORT STORY

ARPAN DEY

Contents

Introduction   *vii*

  1. The Adventure Of The Injured Cabman   1

  2. The Last Lure   27

About The Author   33

The Adventure Of The Injured Cabman is a Sherlock Holmes adventure by Arpan Dey, an enthralling story that retains the original flavor of Conan Doyle's famous detective. The book contains one more short story by Arpan Dey: The Last Lure. Suitable for kids and adults alike, the latter story can be interpreted in many ways, and has a deep meaning within. The Sherlock Holmes adventure is packed with action, adventure, mystery and important lessons.

Introduction

Life is a bonus gift. It is a few years we have temporarily borrowed (don't ask me from whom). Many number of strange, intriguing and even intimidating thoughts chase the mind of a young person (and an old person as well). And memory is not a failsafe way to store them.

As a young person who has been confronted with the above problem, I found it best to let others know of my thoughts and perspectives. But inherently, I am an introvert. And it would a very uninteresting read indeed if I directly jotted down my ideas pointwise. So I decided to write. I couldn't manage a serious novel along with my studies and other activities. So I chose short stories instead.

I have always loved reading short stories. It is a different feeling altogether that reading no novel can produce. Short stories almost always have some unexpected ending, and some questions remain unanswered, which are left to the reader's imagination.

From a very young age, I loved detective stories. So I always knew there would be at least one detective story in my collection, if ever I decide to write short stories. The Adventures of the Injured Cabman is a detective story written on the lines of Sir Arthur Conan Doyle's famous Sherlock Holmes, the detective whose intellect and philosophy has inspired and enlightened me to an unimaginably huge extent. Although the names and identity of Conan Doyle's characters have been retained, no copyright infringement is intended by my story.

Included also is a fantasy allegory – The Last Lure – a story about a psychopath and a magical book.

So that's all, pretty much. Each story is unique in its own way. I hope that this collection of two short stories (the Sherlock Holmes story is not *that* short) – which can be perhaps called a book, rather boldly – succeeds in enlightening the reader and offering him/her some enjoyable moments.

Author

2020

ONE

THE ADVENTURE OF THE INJURED CABMAN

"Life is but an accident of combination, Watson. And yet, and yet... is it not shameful that we devote so less time to a subject of such importance? Look out of the window – the people move about their daily business, blissfully unaware that their very existence is paradoxical. Deduction is one thing, Watson, as I have already had occasion to tell you. I simply obtain particular results from general ones. But look at your immediate surroundings. It is all so specific, so particular, so complex. Do we not need to do the reverse? Obtain general result about the nature of reality from this knowledge, or at least try to?"

"Induction," I remarked. "In mathematics, we indeed can prove general results from particular ones, Holmes. Only yesterday I was reading an article on the subject."

"Tut, tut, the same old Watson. Mathematical induction is based on assumptions. It is one thing to prove a mathematical statement, and another to comment on the fundamental nature of reality. Unfortunately, neither you nor I have the expertise to do so."

It was morning, and my companion was having his breakfast. At the time, I was married. But since my wife was away for some days, we were, once more, residing in our old Baker Street rooms together. The record of this incident somehow escaped my notice for a long time. There is no particular reason for secrecy about the case, since the primary character is no more alive. However, the case was so strange and singular, that both I and my companion are of the opinion that if I am to lay down, before the public, a narrative once more, then this would be a very good choice. Holmes earned little from the case, and many other cases have offered greater fields for the peculiar talents of Holmes. And yet, all in all, the case that I am about to lay down before my long-suffering readers forms a great narrative, and demonstrates once more the methods of perhaps the only self-employed consultant detective in the world.

I was seated opposite to him, listening to his lecture, wondering about the diverse trains of thoughts which constantly ran through his great mind. Sherlock Holmes was in a serious philosophical mood that morning. It was not often that I found him in such a mood. This side of his personality was in sharp contrast to the lounging cocaine-addict that he was in times when life was listless for him.

"My dear fellow, my dear fellow, I really do regret the death of the late-lamented Moriarty. Such a mind is exceedingly rare, and as long as that man dwelled in our midst, there could be no loss of singular cases. Alas, today, the faculties are starved. The old days are gone, my dear Watson, we have stagnated. In spite of your medical advice, one with a brain like mine must resort to artificial stimulants in such times."

I looked at the cocaine bottle with a sense of foreboding. I knew it was useless to argue with him. I noticed the tinge of pride that he expressed in his speech. Of course, he has the right to pride himself on his brain, for he really plays the game just for the game's sake. He has never overdone either humility or conceit. To the ideal reasoner, he would say, a fact should be interpreted exactly as it is, in all its bearings.

It was clear to me that Holmes was to revert back to his old addiction once more, when I saw a most beautiful sight before my eyes. Lestrade, the Scotland Yard detective, was stepping out of a cab, right in front of our rooms. His appearance must mean ill news to some relative of a murdered man, or to the owner of a stolen artifact, I said to myself. But at the moment, all I was aware of was that it meant a new case for Holmes. The wheels would move once more, and once more I would be given a chance to study his methods. That was all I cared for.

Holmes sat up in his armchair, and I took my seat. The detective entered, looking very weary.

"Mr. Holmes. How do you do? Terrible business, terrible. I came here right from the place of the crime itself. I am at my wit's end, Mr. Holmes," Lestrade said breathlessly.

"Calm down, Lestrade," said the commanding voice. "From the state of your clothes I gather that the thing, whatever it is, has occurred on the road?"

"You are right, Mr. Holmes. Near Tottenham Court Road. Terrible business. A cabman was shot some time ago. Two bullets right inside. I would be surprised if he lives at all. According to the witnesses, two men, aged about thirty or five-and-thirty, shot the cabman all of a sudden, and vanished into one of the lanes."

Holmes sat up straight with interest. "And they weren't caught?"

"Most of the people were afraid, but a couple chased 'em into the lane. But they lost the men. I immediately reached the spot and the man has been taken to the Scotland Yard hospital. I was only wondering, and I am sure Mr. Holmes would agree, that the remarkable thing is how desperate the men were. Firing in broad daylight! Must be some deep old enmity. What do you make of it?"

"As Dr. Watson here knows, I do not give opinions before gathering the facts. I take it that there is little to be learned from the road. All the same, I would like to visit the place once. Soon. And is the man in a position to talk?"

"I should think not. But I will ask you to come down to the hospital as soon as he can talk."

"One last question. Did you trace where the cab was before the incident, or to where it was going? Also, I take it that there were no passengers in the cab at the time?"

"No passengers, of course. And I admit, Mr. Holmes, that I don't quite see the point in trying to find the answer to your former question. How can it matter where he was coming from or going to? Mr. Holmes, the Yard doesn't need you to tell at least this that the man was a long-standing enemy of the assailants."

"Good morning, Lestrade. I will go to the spot at once. And as a friendly advice, you might be thinking on wrong lines. Would you like to accompany me, Watson?"

"I would be glad to do so, if I can be of any help," I replied. I was experiencing the old feeling in my guts once more. What a strange life was his, I wondered. One moment, he comments on the fundamental nature of reality. The next moment, he prepares himself for a period of hibernation, with his artificial stimulant. The next moment, he is the man of action again.

"How could you be sure that Lestrade was wrong in the old-enmity theory?" I could not help asking in the cab, on our way to the place of the crime. He was seated quietly beside me, with knitted brows. I half-expected an angry outburst of impatience from him, but fortunately he chose to answer my question.

"My dear Watson, is that not obvious?"

"I confess that I miss the point."

"If it were a matter of old enmity, they could have planned and attacked in some more suitable time. Why so desperate? Why attack on open road, in broad daylight? Could this fact be explained by Lestrade's theory? No, no Watson, my instincts are against this theory. There was some urgent need to kill the man, or maybe something else. Do you follow?"

"Yes, I see it now. It is obvious."

Our cab stopped near the place of the incident, in Tottenham Court Road. It was easy to see that something was amiss, since a large crowd had gathered near the place. Holmes clenched his fists in contempt. "How can I ever read anything from that mess? Why can't the official force be a bit more sensible?"

At any rate, we went forward, pushing through the crowd of curious people. The cab was lying on its side. We gathered that the driver lost his control on being shot, and the cab toppled over sideways, as a result. The men fired from the right, and the cab toppled toward the left. All that remained to see was a small pool of dark-red blood to the right of the cab, on the road. Holmes bent down and examined the blood for a long time. Finally, he sighed and stood up. Without showing any further interest in his surroundings, he walked back to the cab. "Scotland Yard," he said to our cabman.

The Yard was in a state of uproar when we arrived. "Mr. Holmes, Mr. Holmes," Lestrade came running toward us, out of breath. "He is gone."

"The injured cabman?"

"Yes. The doctor didn't even get a chance to examine him. The staff only bandaged the injured places. Why, he might already be dead, given his condition. The guard went away for a bit, and in that interval, somebody must have carried him away."

"From a hospital surrounded by Scotland Yard officials?"

"Exactly, Mr. Holmes. That is what bothers me. This case goes deeper than I thought at first. But to tell you the truth, he was put in the newly-constructed ward, and it is not as heavily-guarded there. For one thing, there were no other patients or doctors except him at that ward. And he was in the ground floor, so it was not a difficult matter to carry him off."

"Or to escape?"

"Sorry?"

"Couldn't it be that he simply escaped? Maybe he thought that his pursuers would track him here, maybe he thought he wasn't safe even here?"

"Are you crazy? He has two bullets in his body, how can he escape all by himself? He might even be dead, Mr. Holmes."

"Didn't you notice any stranger entering that building?"

"Not that I am aware of. And many strangers visit the hospitals daily."

Holmes nodded his head impatiently. "Well, well, nothing further can be done right now. Let me know if there are any updates. Good day to you."

As we were about to get into our cab, a man came running toward us. "Sir," he addressed Lestrade. "I found this note on the bed of the man." It was a short note from a so-called "well-wisher", stating that the man was dead, and his body had been carried out of the hospital for burial. No good can come from searching for him further.

The ward was immediately searched, but with no results. "Are you sure the note was present from the time the man was missing? How could you miss noticing it? Could it not be that someone slipped in the note soon afterward, but not at the time when the man was removed?," Lestrade asked the man who had brought the note.

"No sir, I can't tell exactly. But it may have escaped my notice the first time, so disturbed was I on discovering that the man is gone."

"So this man discovered first that the man is gone," remarked Holmes after the man had gone. "Is he reliable?"

"Absolutely, Mr. Holmes. He has been in the force for over fourteen years now," answered Lestrade.

"Well then, there is not much to be gathered from this note. All I can see is that the ink hasn't dried, so it was written quite recently. The writer has tried to feign his handwriting, since there is frequent overwriting in so short a note, and some of the letters don't match up everywhere. It is impossible to say which is his original handwriting, but likely these type of 'w's are a part of his original writing, since the occurrence is so less, and has been over-written on, in two places. But that doesn't tell us much. We can't get a specimen of this person's original writing, since we don't even know him. But then, though this doesn't give us much particulars, one thing is obvious. I wouldn't have missed this case for Moriarty. My dear Watson," he suddenly realized the presence of his silent companion. "I perceive a deception. This promises to be an interesting case... But for now, Watson, we will give ourselves up to music. The violin awaits me in our humble rooms located in a small street under this broad sky, by the name of Baker Street."

Among the so many gifts that my companion is gifted with, I have been most amazed by his power of mental detachment. No matter how pressing a matter was at hand, he could always detach himself completely for some time. I was immersed in these thoughts, watching him whiling away the time, with his violin. He was an exceptionally-talented violin player when he was in good spirits. The soothing music indeed made the incident of the morning appear like some nightmare to me.

"You want to discuss the case, do you not?" asked Holmes, once he was done playing his violin.

"Well, I see that my restlessness gave me away."

"Watson, Watson, don't tell me that you have understood nothing, after spending these years with me? What do you make of it?"

"I must say, I share Lestrade's perplexity. An innocent cabman is shot in broad daylight. The assailants escape. Then the man himself disappears from the hospital. Then there is this mysterious note. The motive of the crime is also shrouded in mystery. I can make neither head nor tail of this business, and that is my final word. Why, Holmes, everything in this matter is just as far away from the expected as can be."

"You are right, it is bizarre. And that is precisely why it should be easier to reach a conclusion. Do not look surprised, Watson. What have I told you repeatedly? Bizarre happenings narrow down the field of possibilities."

"My dear Holmes, I don't quite follow you sometimes."

"Take, for example, the theft of Sir Henry Baskerville's one boot. It was a bizarre incident, but it was also clear, was it not my dear Watson, that the thief didn't steal the boot to wear, since then he would have taken two boots? Also, he returned the new one and took the old one, making it plain that he needed the odor of the owner, and a dog was involved in the case. Had he been more cunning, he would not have returned the new one, or else he could take both the boots. We could not rule out the possibility of petty theft then. The more commonplace an incident is, the more difficult it is to investigate. And what great proof can one require, than the fact that life in itself is so complicated, and so commonplace. After a few days at most, I fancy, this case will finish, and I will be left once more, in the state which you so despise. How can I, then, ignore my cocaine bottle? The world moves on, Watson. The detectives fight to rise in the Yard, you strive to increase your practice, every people out there strive to succeed in his profession. And here am I, left with nothing but powers with no regular field to exert them upon."

It was not common to see Holmes drift into such talks in the midst of a case. Had he already formed his conclusions? Or had he mentally decided to drop the case? Where was that active man, charging and recharging his pipe with tobacco and thinking hard with knitted brows?

"Holmes, what do you make of the case?"

"I am no maker of suspense films. But I should have thought that the conclusions were very clear and obvious. For one, I believe there is some strong deception. I would not, for instance, be surprised to find that perhaps there was no murder attempt at all."

"But, Holmes! The people saw it, how..."

"Well, well. That can all be arranged. Of course, two people did fire at the cabman, but whether the bullets really injured him, or whether they were indeed enemies, is something I could not say. Moreover, as Lestrade said, the doctor didn't have occasion to examine him."

"But, this is impossible. The blood!"

"My dear Watson, as a doctor, what do you say? Can blood be distinguished from hemoglobin from a distance?"

"No. From a distance, they look alike."

"From close?"

"Then, hemoglobin can be distinguished. But to the trained eye. Why, do you think that was hemoglobin lying on the road?"

"I couldn't examine it closely. But did the color occur normal to you?"

"I did not see it minutely, Holmes. But it appeared darker than blood."

"Deoxygenated blood can be darker, of course. But that is not the only point. There are other reasons as well to believe that the incident was not as straightforward as you think."

"What do you mean, my dear Holmes?"

"The cab toppled over sideways, toward the left. As soon as the cabman was shot, I presume. Then how is it that there were no blood stains anywhere on the cab, and a neat pool of blood some considerable distance to the right of the cab?"

"Holmes!"

"Exactly, Watson, exactly. It is the custom of the detectives to overlook such things. They don't even try to picture the incident in their minds. Then they could easily perceive the loophole. And that is not all. What troubles me is the note. What even is the purpose of the note? If the criminals wanted to take away the man, why would they leave an unnecessary note as a clue behind?"

"I had not thought of that."

"What could be the purpose of such a note, except to waste time, paper and ink? What purpose comes to your mind, Watson?"

"To try to convince the Yard to not continue their search, perhaps?"

"Do you think someone as tenacious as Lestrade would stop his search in account of a single note? No, no Watson. Try again."

"What then? To inform that the man was dead. But what good would that mean to them?"

"Exactly. From the very beginning, don't you think that things are overdone? A cab topples over? If I were to shoot you while you were driving a cab, at most you would have lost control and maybe veer away sideways. But topple over? And then, we have this note. I think the motive of the criminal or criminals is to prove that that particular cabman is dead."

"But Holmes! How could the cabman intentionally topple his cab over while sitting on it? The incident took place in front of many witnesses..."

"And that is precisely why I think that they wanted the public to know that the man was dead. Else, why murder in the day, in a public place?"

"But again, how in the name of the devil could the cabman intentionally topple his cab over while driving it?"

"Ah, that is not a serious flaw in my theory. The assailants could have shot the left wheel, and maybe pushed the cab leftward from the side, while firing. The sound of two pistol shots would have driven the senses out of half the witnesses. All they would see is two people forcing their way in the cab and shooting the cabman. The cab, as it appears, loses control and topples over."

"But if they wanted to prove that the man was dead, would they have killed him? Else, how could they do it? The man couldn't pretend to be dead since his body would be examined."

"Exactly Watson. That is where I am stuck presently. I could suggest possible solutions, but they appear to be so less trustworthy, that I doubt whether the criminals would rely on them."

"Like what?"

"Well, the criminals could have accomplices among the crowd. They could pretend to be doctors and announce that the man was dead, or maybe on some pretext take him to some hospital and later announce him to be dead. Maybe that he was buried quietly and so."

"All that seems so..."

"I know, I know. But let that be our present working hypothesis for want of a better one. If all else is impossible, as I have bored you by telling so, whatever remains, regardless of whether it is likely or not, must be the truth. One thing is certain. The cabman is the center of this mystery. He, for some reason, wants the world to know that he is dead. Maybe he could then live under a false identity, or go into hiding for some time. But why, why..."

"Well, he wants to throw off some pursuer?"

"That is the most obvious solution. But that is not exhaustive. Other possibilities remain. And then, how terrible can a pursuer be to arrange for such a desperate situation? No, Watson. For the first time, I feel that this case is indeed..."

"Holmes, you have failed before. We all have."

"Yes, yes. But those cases were glaringly obvious. Maybe there was no legal crime at all, or I couldn't capture the criminal, which in any case is not my business. But here, following a logical train of deductions, we reach extremely unlikely conclusions. Of course, we must have to accept our results for now, and yet, this case does not only initially look strange. It remains bizarre from every perspective."

"So what do we do next?"

"There lies the problem. Luck has thrown in our way a beautiful little problem. But there is no solid material on which to proceed. We have no idea as to this cabman, or his assailants. All we know is not sufficient to take further action, I daresay. I would wait for some time, to see if the official force can throw any light upon the matter. Else, let us push it to the back of our minds. For once, let us follow our Lestrade's advice. It is no good spinning theories sitting here, especially when there is so little material."

"But, Holmes, why should this man trumpet the fact that he is dead, in such a manner? He could seek protection from the Yard perhaps, if he is afraid of some pursuer."

Holmes did not reply. "Holmes, maybe they could have bribed the guard and taken the man from the hospital?"

"Either way, Watson, there is nothing much we could do. For now, I say we direct our thoughts to more cheerful lines. That is, if I am not much mistaken, Mrs. Hudson coming up with the food."

And again, I saw the transition from the active logical reasoner to the musician with brooding eyes. For the next two days, he would not often leave his armchair, absorbed in music and philosophy. Lestrade visited us in the afternoon of the second day, but without any news. On the third day, luck favored us at last. It was painful for me to see my companion stuck with the case in such a manner.

Holmes had spent much of these last few days beside the window. On the third day, he finally dropped his violin and looked at me with some interest. "There is a young lad there. I have been observing him for the last two days. It is clear to me that he is watching our rooms."

I walked over to the window. On the opposite footpath stood a young, clean-shaven and plainly-dressed man, aged about a five-and-twenty years. He indeed seemed to be keeping an eye in our direction. "Holmes...," I began, but he was gone.

Soon, a haggard-looking ruffian emerged from his room. Familiar as I was to his disguises, I couldn't help admiring him. He beckoned me to come toward him, made me wear his dress, overcoat and hat. After a short make-up of my face, I almost exactly resembled the actual form of the ruffian who stood beside me. My role was clear. "Watson, the lad was away just before some time, for a while. I can convince him that I entered this house in that time. I will be going out and befriending him. Maybe this will lead us nowhere, but I will try it all the same. You are to stand near the window and if required, shout out a few words to me. Just make sure that the young man there notices you, and believes that Sherlock Holmes is home."

With my heart beating with excitement, I walked up to the window, trying to follow my friend's attitude to the best of my abilities. The ruffian exited our house. There was no need for me to shout, for the young lad had clearly noticed me. I saw the ruffian walk up to him, and down the street together. Relieved, and somewhat tensed, I returned to my chair.

The whole day I waited expectantly for my companion's return. However, he only returned late in the night.

"I have identified the cabman, Watson. It is the same man."

"Which man?"

"Oh. You were not here at the time. This man came to consult me. Think for a moment, Watson, how you would feel if a man whom you do not know was to stick to you like shadow, go wherever you went, and sit in front of your house all night."

"Was someone following him, then?"

"Yes. And following openly. Sticking to him literally. He even told me that the man had followed him on his way to my rooms. However, I was not convinced by his story."

"Why?"

"Well, for one, he visited me on foot, being a cabman. For another, I could spot other inconsistencies in his story. It was clear to me, when the man asked me to visit his place one night, that this was some plan to get me out of the way, when some crime was to take place. I naturally declined to act. Now I see that I was mistaken. Someone was indeed pursuing him, and maybe this same person has a hand in the incident we are presently investigating."

Next morning, in the breakfast table, he was as absorbed as ever. I could not get him to speak more of his adventures of the day before. After the breakfast, he informed me that the man had been recaptured and he was off to the hospital. He asked me whether I cared to come, and I naturally accompanied him.

In front of the hospital, I was somewhat surprised to find that same young lad waiting. He was wearing a mask, which he later revealed was due to his fear of infection in the hospital. Holmes approached him and shook hands. "Jeff told me that you are a young detective interested in the case of the cabman," said Holmes to the lad. "The man was recaptured, and he informed us both of it. Let us go in and see him, then."

"Nicholas Chen," said the lad. "I have heard of you, Mr. Holmes, and would love to study your methods and make use of this very fortunate chance."

We shook hands and continued, accompanied by Lestrade.

"So, what do you say about the case, Mr. Holmes? Have you formed an opinion yet?"

"No, Mr. Chen. I daresay not."

We entered the ward, and followed Chen to the bed. The cabman was lying on the bed, in a pitiful condition. Holmes introduced myself and Chen.

After the interview was over, Holmes wanted to have a word with the cabman, alone. We all gathered outside the hospital, waiting for him. He soon emerged, and took me and Chen aside.

"Mr. Chen, if you would allow me to say so, I would like to have a word with you in my rooms."

"Well, I don't see how would that be of any help to you, since I only gathered the particulars of the case yesterday and have not yet formed any conclusions, like yourself. But surely I would come if you would like."

We drove back to our Baker Street rooms, accompanied by Chen, who looked somewhat pale. In the cab, he kept shooting furtive glances at Holmes.

"Mr. Chen, to start with, would you mind introducing your true self to us? This here, as you might already know, is Dr. Watson. You may speak as freely in front of him as you would do in front of myself."

"What's all this, Mr. Holmes? I am Nicholas Chen, a detective..."

"My time is of importance, and if you would rather choose not to speak the truth, I daresay the matter will forever pass beyond the little and futile powers I have been so fortunately able to acquire. Watson, as you know, my suspicions were aroused by the fact that this young man here has taken the trouble to keep an watch over our rooms, for the last two days. Since I am not involved in any other cases right now, it seemed reasonable to me that this man might be connected to the incident at hand. So, I dressed up like a ruffian and went to befriend him, while Watson here played the role of Sherlock Holmes, looking down from his windows."

"It was you, you Mr. Holmes?"

"I introduced myself as Jeff, a ruffian living near the Yard hospital. I invented the story that Sherlock Holmes wanted to talk to Jeff, and asked the latter to try to gather news about the disappearance of the cabman from the hospital. Chen, for want of the real name, asked me to do the same – gather news about the cabman. Then, I pretended that I myself was bribed to dislocate the man, and that I knew his location. Chen offered me a huge sum of money to know the location. I believe he was also very satisfied that I had not told this crucial piece of information to Sherlock Holmes. I pretended to fall for the money. It was arranged that I and my men would smuggle the man back into the hospital, since I lied to Chen that we had two Yard officials in our confidences. I also convinced Chen that I will just let Holmes know that he had been caught and ask him to visit the hospital, since Holmes would get to know the information anyhow."

"My dear Holmes!" I could not help crying out.

"Then, I proceeded to the cab office, gathered the address of the cabman in question, and dropped a letter for him. It was clear to me that this cabman must be a nervous sort of man, and I learned that he is a psychological patient. Obsessive compulsive disorder, Watson."

"Yes," I replied. "It is a dangerous disorder. Coupled with foniasophobia or persecution complex, it can result into acts like this. I gather that this cabman was afraid of being murdered. And his mental disorders magnified his fears to such a state that he devised this incomplete and rather unwise plan of shooting himself in the midst of a crowded road and feign death."

"Exactly, Watson. He came to me to drive me off, so that I do not discover the fact that he is still alive. There has been no such pursuer as he described. That any criminal could devise such a plan, and yet not observe the fact that he could not possibly feign death in front of a crowd of curious people, seemed to suggest invariably that the cabman was not in a normal state of mind. At any rate, I gathered, thus, that he must be a nervous man and must be on the look-out for letters. So I addressed a letter to him, stating that I have discovered his secret and it would do him no harm to come back to the hospital. It would be arranged with the Yard. Fortunately, he accepted my advice, and so today Jeff could pretend to have brought back the man. He was so nervous a man that he actually hid the letter under his bandage."

"But Lestrade, Holmes?"

"Ah. I had to tell everything to old Lestrade, and that the cabman could not possibly be arrested for his deed, though they were not completely legal, of course. Lestrade agreed to cooperate."

"But Mr. Holmes? What have I to do anything with all these? Yes, I am a young detective, so on seeing the so-called Jeff emerge from the house of the famous Sherlock Holmes, and on seeing that he himself approached me, I naturally wanted to find out the location of the cabman. Your talent is recognized, Holmes. Everyone at the Yard knows you, reveres you. But my profession is still in its infancy. Why should I leave a chance? But what do you mean by all this? I have absolutely nothing to do with the matter."

"On the contrary, you have everything to do with the matter."

"Mr. Holmes!"

"Why were you watching over our rooms?"

"I kept a watch over your house simply because I was on the lookout for a chance to speak to you."

"You waited outside for two days, for that reason? And you have not introduced yourself yet."

"Alright, alright. I am Francis Blackwood. I feigned my identity. But you have, Mr. Holmes, absolutely no evidence that I have anything to do with the matter. Can you prove it?"

"Ah. The same old pride. Clean job, right? That's what you call it? But then, if you are so certain, could you, Mr. Blackwood, take the trouble to explain why you were so anxious today at the hospital, that the cabman should not recognize you? Besides wearing a mask, you went to the extent of combing your hair in an entirely different way. That changes a person's appearance dramatically. If only you would have known that Jeff himself was none other than Holmes, who had already observed your true hairstyle, you would perhaps have not taken this unwise action?"

"I do not understand. I wore the mask to protect myself from infection in the hospital, since my health is fragile."

"And you changed your hairstyle for the same reason?"

Blackwood was silenced by this question. The question almost had a magical effect on him. He was gradually losing his defiance. He had perhaps understood that his game was up. To cap it all, Holmes's next question came.

"Could you also explain to me, how and why did you walk right up to the cabman's bed today at the hospital?

Remember, you were leading us. And there were three patients, all covered up in bandages. And you yourself told that you were a young detective, and know nothing much about the matter. Then how did you recognize the cabman from the three patients? Does this not prove that you knew each other?"

"I... I..."

"Instead of inventing another lie, Mr. Blackwood, I would suggest you tell us your true story."

Blackwood broke down miserably before the strong evidence that Holmes had produced. He perhaps understood that his best chance would be to confess everything.

"I will tell you, Mr. Holmes, I will tell you everything."

Holmes stretched himself out on his armchair, with drooping eye-lids and put his fingertips together, ready to listen to our companion's tale.

"I was born in a circus. I was an orphan from my very birth, Mom was gone soon after I was born. My father was gone long ago. He had left me plenty, and one of my uncles, who was a professor of science, encouraged me to pursue science. I used to do a lot of study on my own, Mr. Holmes, though I was also an acrobat in the circus. I enjoyed the life in the circus. I was, on the whole, well-off. The closest I ever had to my father was one of his friends, Mr. Price, who also worked in the circus. I loved and respected him as much as my father, if not more. He had no children, and naturally treated me as his own son. We were living happily together in the circus. When the fantasies of childhood faded away, my uncle soon wanted to take me away from the circus for education. It was very difficult for me to decide, Mr. Holmes. But in the end, I chose education. The night before my departure, Price took me aside and told me something,

Mr. Holmes, which changed me forever."

"Pray continue your narrative."

"Mr. Holmes, at the time, as you may already know, there operated a very dangerous criminal gang in London. They specialized in smuggling illegal drugs. My father's best friend, Mr. Holmes, he developed hypoxia and went mad. He was hospitalized. During a critical operation, he suddenly developed breathing problems. A very crucial lifesaving drug was stolen from the hospital, and the theft was not discovered in time. The doctors had to waste considerable time in acquiring the drug while operating on him, and due to the delay, he - he went mad, permanently. My father couldn't forget it. He vowed to revenge his friend's madness. He entered the gang with the intention of disrupting the entire organization, pretending to be a criminal, a worthy gang member. However, such gangs have spies everywhere. His secret was discovered, and he was cruelly, pitilessly murdered before even I was born. You would not understand how I felt on discovering this from Price. I almost went mad with rage and grief at the time. Soon, I calmed down. Price told me more. My father had told Price, secretly, some days before his death, that should he die, a dangerous member of the gang, who also happened to be a cabman, would be responsible for his death. Also, a man from our own circus happened to be involved with the gang. My father told everything to Price, and he to me. I know the gang operates no more at that level now, but some part of it has survived still. From that day on, Mr. Holmes, I vowed to stick to this man day and night. But he appeared to be no less cunning. Never could I see him meeting any unknown man, or any cabman for that matter. Perhaps he could sense something. But I waited patiently, ready to strike at slightest notice."

Blackwood stopped his narrative, and gulped down some water.

"But patience did win at last. A few weeks ago, I saw, with my own eyes, Mr. Holmes, that this man was in conversation with a cabman. The same cabman, in fact, who now lies in the Yard hospital. I did not strike immediately. I waited patiently, and saw that this man went back to the same cabman, time and again. Little doubt remained in my mind that this was the man who was responsible for the death of poor father. Vengeance swelled inside me uncontrollably. I wanted to tear the man apart, limb to limb, then and there. But something told me to wait. I wanted to see and relish him die, gradually and slowly. That would be better a punishment than if I killed him instantly."

"And yet, Mr. Blackwood, you failed to realize that even death is not the ultimate punishment."

"That's what Price said. My father, according to him, did not want to kill the enemies. But he could not make them mad. Have you ever had the chance to witness any of your close friends go mad? They stare at you and don't even recognize you. That is worse than death."

"At any rate, please continue."

"I began to put letters into his house at night, slip chits into his cab – reminding him how he had wronged me and asking him to prepare for his death. He caught me in such acts twice, and we were face-to-face. But I openly challenged him, and he did not try to hold me further. I think he is a nervous sort of man, the devil that he is. He was convinced that I would not rest before killing him. So he was always very afraid. Serves him right, though."

Holmes sat up straight. "Mr. Blackwood, what you have done certainly does not elevate your position in your father's eyes."

"I know, I know, but..."

"Not that. You have terrified an innocent man. The cabman was never in any way concerned with the gang of which you speak, or with your father's death either."

"Mr. Holmes!"

"Yes. I am aware of the gang. The gang operated under the supervision of a Professor Moriarty. He acted as a supervisor and advisor to numerous such gangs, and perhaps remains the most dangerous man who ever lived. But I disclosed him, and he is dead now. I followed the newspaper closely regarding any news of the gangs after his death. As Dr. Watson here knows, I was myself on an exile at the time, and the world believed me to be dead too. I read the news of the murder of a cabman, by a member of the gang. No doubt, he was killed for some reason, by someone of his own gang, as is common in such organizations. It is beyond question that this is the cabman you intended to kill. A thorough study of the record of the man who now lies in the Yard hospital has showed clearly that his history is clean, except for the fact that he is a psychological patient. That is why his fears caused his otherwise quick-witted mind to plan such a tragedy with two of his closest friends. Due to his psychological shortcomings I presume, however, he left a few loopholes in his singular plan. Thus, from the beginning it was clear to me that there has been no murder attempt. Two men shot at his cab, but no bullets penetrated his body. Some blood-like substance, perhaps hemoglobin, was spread on the road. He planned to feign death, or something of the sort. However, the quick appearance of Lestrade on the scene prevented him from executing his plan. He was carried off to the Yard hospital, from where he managed to escape somehow, since his ward was not heavily-guarded. He needed to escape, since otherwise the doctor would have found out that there has been no injuries at all."

"Mr. Holmes? You terrify me. Am I to learn that I chased an innocent person for the last few days?"

"As you have no doubt perceived, your position is a questionable one in the eyes of law. For how long have you chased this poor man?"

"Eight-and-twenty days, Mr. Holmes. How can I ever be easy again? What can I say to my own conscience?"

I could see that Blackwood was shaken by this news. Holmes sat quietly for a long time, absent-mindedly smoking his pipe. After what seemed to be an exceptionally long time, Holmes stood up.

"Mr. Blackwood, I have reasons to believe that your story is true. And had the time period been greater than twenty-eight days, I would have had to reconsider my decision. The advantage of not being part of the regular force, Watson, is that though there is no fame and money, I need not follow strict rules. I am my own judge, and can be flexible in my decisions. The door is not locked, Mr. Blackwood."

"Oh, Mr. Holmes, I can't thank you enough for understanding."

"You will go and apologize to the cabman, and promise never to bother him in the future again."

"But..."

"I will arrange it with the official detectives."

"Of course, Mr. Holmes."

"I know that the cabman was mentally unsound for a long time. If it gets any worse due to your actions, however, I must make the matter public. I can't help it any longer then. Till then, you will be constantly followed by a Yard official."

Blackwood seemed troubled, but nodded at last.

"Do you realize that the man from your circus, who was a part of the gang, intentionally met with this innocent cabman to throw yourself off his track and onto the tracks of the innocent cabman? You will do all you can to trace down and lure the criminal from the circus, into the hands of the Yard."

Blackwood nodded firmly, and swept from the room.

"Is it not strange, my dear Watson, that Moriarty can supply us with fresh cases even now, so many years after his death? Such was the terrible organization he had formed. Not a clue to the mastermind behind it. Many people are waiting to strike now, just like young Blackwood. So I daresay we must thank Moriarty even now. The after-effects of his actions are far from over."

I could not help but agree. Indeed, had it not been for Holmes, London would have been in the vice-like grip of that man to this day. What devilish intellect!

"There indeed seems to exist an overall effect of constancy. Most criminals whom the law cannot touch, are not happy at mind. And some die in the hands of their own comrades. Indeed, what a strange world we live in. There are so many kinds of people roaming about, Watson. Singular incidents are taking place every minute, as is inevitable when so many people choose to live together in this beautiful and diverse planet."

I knew that he was preparing to be the lazy cocaine-addict once more. How singular a man he himself was, I wondered. He lives his entire life hoping for such small chances to employ his ice-cold logical reasoning to solve real-life problems. Soon after a case is over, he would again go into hibernation, thinking about human psychology, the futility of life, and the nature of reality, while caressing his violin – his only companion which allowed him to leave the material world for a small interval of time. He sat with his chin on his hand, gazing at the little part of the beautiful sky that was visible through the small window.

TWO

THE LAST LURE

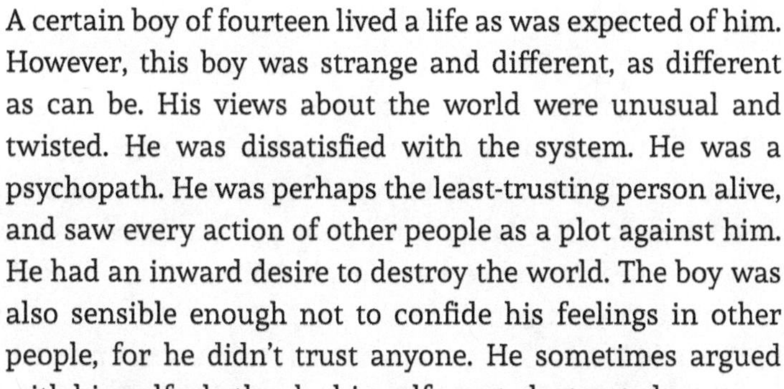

A certain boy of fourteen lived a life as was expected of him. However, this boy was strange and different, as different as can be. His views about the world were unusual and twisted. He was dissatisfied with the system. He was a psychopath. He was perhaps the least-trusting person alive, and saw every action of other people as a plot against him. He had an inward desire to destroy the world. The boy was also sensible enough not to confide his feelings in other people, for he didn't trust anyone. He sometimes argued with himself whether he himself was to be trusted.

If I tell others, he thought furiously, they will either take me to be a lunatic or lecture on a 'positive outlook on life'. He sneered. Trying to change humans and the system is foolish and pointless, he said to himself. If you wanted to survive in such a world, there is only one way – to change yourself. But I would never do that. That's like losing to the system. If only I had the power, the boy found himself thinking desperately, I could show them. I could rip everyone of them limb to limb. People would perhaps say that that was wrong, evil. But he knew better. There is no good, there is no evil; there is only power. Those unable to resist it must succumb. The fittest survives.

The boy concluded that there was only one way to punish humankind, and that was to destroy the entire world. He knew he would die if he succeeded, but he was ready to die for so noble a cause. He was even half-curious to find out what happened after death. Of course, everything is expected to end after death, but you can never know for sure without dying.

But that is impossible, thought the boy. I am not a President. I don't have nuclear weapons at my command. How can I destroy the world? Soon, the boy became obsessed with this. He could very well understand that the feat was impossible. However, he thought wildly, the earth is after all a body spinning away in deep space. From meteors to gamma ray bursters, space poses a lot of threats. What if the earth is destroyed in such a manner? Agreed, I wouldn't do it myself, but my wish would be fulfilled nevertheless. Else, what if I could get my hands on a powerful, deadly and perhaps magical object? Ha, but such objects can't exist, can they?

It could have taken the boy some fifty years to find such an object, if at all possible. But he got lucky, perhaps. The very next month was his birthday. Exhausted, he dozed off early that day. Next morning, he saw that his mother had unwrapped all the presents and thrown away the wrappers. Amidst story books, toys, a watch and birthday cards, the boy found a strange book. It caught his eyes at once.

"Who's that from, mum?"

"No idea. Must be from one of your friends or uncle. I and your dad gave you the watch."

The mysterious book was covered in leather. There were no words on the back cover – no price sticker, no author name, no description. Across the front cover, there were just two words: The Bridger. He opened the book. There was no author name. Then after a few pages, there was a page titled **"Introduction"**. The words were handwritten. He read the shortest introduction to a book ever: "This book bridges the distance between its world and the real world. Use it well."

It's world? Now what was that supposed to mean?

He turned over to the first chapter. It was a story named: **"The Bespectacled Crow"**. Again, the story was handwritten. He read the first paragraph, which described a happy crow, which used to nick food from kitchens. There was a picture – a black crow, mischievous and happy, perched on top of a windowsill. The picture was drawn by hand.

What rubbish is this? Someone must have sent this book as a joke, thought the boy. Bridges the gap between worlds, bespectacled crow, like kids' fairy tales.

However, he continued reading. The other crows sent the happy crow away for some reason. The sad crow flew a great distance away and landed on a deserted road. He found a pair of spectacles lying there. The crow put the specs over its beak, and discovered that it brought far objects nearer. Only if this thing could reveal the thoughts of the other crows to me more closely, thought the crow. And the story ended there. It made no sense, thought the boy. Even fairy tales are better than this. His eyes fell on the picture once more, and he froze.

He distinctly saw that the crow had glasses over its beak now. How could this be a trick of the eyes or the mind? The first time he looked at the picture, the crow had no glasses. And did it look happier then? Was it at a different location then? Does the pictures in this book change to my realization? He felt a sense of foreboding, yet excitement. What else could the book do? And who sent it? *Who?*

He read and examined the other stories. All the pictures changed in the same manner. But there were not many stories in the book. The last half of the book was just empty pages, with **"Notes"** etched across the top. The boy was seized by a sudden idea. He wrote a story, in which one of his rivals at school had managed to break his left arm, on such an empty page. He let the ink dry and forced himself to believe that the story had been there for ages. Then he drew a picture of that boy riding his bicycle with pencil. After sometime, he erased it and drew a picture in which the boy lay across his bicycle, clutching his broken left arm, his face distorted with pain. And then, the boy fell asleep. This had never happened before. It was morning, and the boy had just woken up from a full night's sleep. However, he remained asleep till evening.

The boy figured out the reason behind this by himself, while his mother lectured on sleeping early. The book used his mind power to bridge the gap between its world and the real world. The book used his mind power, depriving him temporarily of his consciousness, to make the incident really occur in the real world. The boy should have realized the dangers of the object he was using, but he did not. He was eagerly waiting for news, and sure enough, that evening his rival had fallen from his bicycle and broken his left arm.

The excited boy tried a few more such experiments. He noticed that the bigger the incident was, the longer he fell asleep. Finally, he vowed to use the book for his last wish – to destroy the world. If this didn't work, nothing would. He wasn't sure whether the book could pull off this great feat, but he lured himself into believing that it was possible. He threw caution to the winds and wrote a story anyway, at the end of which the earth is destroyed by a meteor.

The boy half-knew what would happen next, and he was ready for it. The pencil slid off his grip as he finished his drawing. He had barely any strength left. His head dropped on the table, and he peacefully drifted off to a sleep from which he was never going to wake up.

About The Author

Arpan Dey is currently a science student at Delhi Public School, Burdwan (which is a small town in West Bengal, India). He is interested in physics, mathematics and metaphysics (particularly in quantum mechanics, chaos theory, loop quantum gravity, consciousness etc.). He has published some of his science articles (original research and review) with Young Scientists Journal, where he also works as senior physics editor. He has been a young member of the New York Academy of Sciences and has published a popular science book on physics, consciousness and metaphysics, which is available for purchase internationally. He runs a physics blogging site, The Journal of Young Physicists, where students can submit their physics articles for review and publication. He also uploads videos related to physics, mathematics, philosophy, aviation and anything else he finds interesting to his YouTube channel.

In his free time, Arpan likes to read popular science and fiction. He will also be working on educating underprivileged children in villages of West Bengal. He also writes songs, produces music and collaborates with vocalists and producers from around the world to release original songs. He has an official artist channel on YouTube where he releases his music and lyric videos. He has released his debut album titled Unsettled bliss, which contains ten original songs. Although he puts some of his time and efforts into music, he wishes to pursue physics in the future.

His website is at https://arpandey.net.